Will Lila Get the Party She Wants?

"You're not having a party on Saturday!" Jessica said, staring straight at Lila.

"I am so having a party," Lila said.

"Then how come your cook doesn't know anything about it?" Jessica demanded.

"Because . . ." Lila looked down and fidgeted with her French doll. "Because I haven't . . ." Her voice trailed off in a mumble.

"You haven't what?" Elizabeth asked.

Lila defiantly stuck her chin in the air. "I haven't exactly asked my father yet," she admitted. "But since he always says yes, I know I can have the party."

"Oh, brother." Jessica shook her head. "I knew I shouldn't have believed you. You were making all that stuff up."

"I was not," Lila said. "Don't worry. There's going to be a party. And it's going to be great."

Bantam Books in the SWEET VALLEY KIDS series

SWEET VALLEY KIDS

LILA'S APRIL FOOL

Written by
Molly Mia Stewart

Created by
FRANCINE PASCAL

Illustrated by
Ying-Hwa Hu

BANTAM BOOKS
NEW YORK·TORONTO·LONDON·SYDNEY·AUCKLAND

RL 2, 005-008

LILA'S APRIL FOOL
A Bantam Book / April 1994

*Sweet Valley High® and Sweet Valley Kids are
trademarks of Francine Pascal*

Conceived by Francine Pascal

*Produced by Daniel Weiss Associates, Inc.
33 West 17th Street
New York, NY 10011*

Cover art by Susan Tang

ISBN: 0-553-48114-2

Published simultaneously in the United States and Canada

Bantam Books are published by Bantam Books, a division of Bantam
Doubleday Dell Publishing Group, Inc. Its trademark, consisting of the
words "Bantam Books" and the portrayal of a rooster, is Registered in
U.S. Patent and Trademark Office and in other countries. Marca
Registrada. Bantam Books, 1540 Broadway, New York, New York 10036.

PRINTED IN THE UNITED STATES OF AMERICA

OPM   0 9 8 7 6 5 4 3 2

To Eric Nelson Forman

LILA'S
APRIL
FOOL

CHAPTER 1

Cinderella

Jessica Wakefield ran out onto the playground, stuck her arms out wide, and twirled around. "Recess!" she shouted. "My favorite class!"

"Don't you wish you could get a grade for it?" her identical twin sister, Elizabeth, asked.

Jessica giggled. "I bet I'd get a better grade than you for once!"

Usually Elizabeth got better grades than Jessica did. Elizabeth enjoyed second grade and tried her best to do well in all her subjects. She always did her homework before playing safari adventures, or reading a book.

Jessica was just the opposite. She thought the best part of school was playing with her friends. She often passed notes in class instead of doing her work. Jessica didn't dream of adventures the way Elizabeth did. Instead Jessica daydreamed about being a movie star, or a princess in disguise.

But even though Jessica and Elizabeth were different on the inside, they looked exactly alike on the outside. Each girl had pretty blue-green eyes and long blond hair with bangs. Being identical twins was special to them. They shared secrets and candy and clothes. They also shared a bedroom with matching beds and identical stuffed koala bears. Sometimes they could even finish each other's sentences. In short, they were best friends.

"What should we play?" Ellen Riteman asked as she, Amy Sutton, and Lila Fowler joined the twins. Ellen looked at Lila for an answer.

Lila liked to be the boss. Her family was one of the wealthiest in Sweet Valley, and he usually let her have her way. Elizabeth didn't like her very much, but Jessica considered Lila her second-best friend.

"I know," Lila said after a moment. "Let's play Cinderella."

"I want to be Cinderella this time," Amy said. "I never get to be Cinderella."

Jessica and Lila looked at each other and giggled.

"What's so funny?" Amy demanded. She glowered at Lila.

"Yeah, why can't Amy be Cinderella?" Elizabeth asked.

"It's her haircut," Lila said in her usual know-it-all way. "Can't you see?"

Amy put one hand on her head. She had just had her hair cut. Now it was as short as a boy's. "What's wrong with it?" she asked as their teacher walked by.

Mrs. Otis stopped walking and smiled down at Amy. "There's nothing wrong with your hair. I like it."

"So why can't I be Cinderella?" Amy asked.

Mrs. Otis looked hard at Jessica and Lila. "I don't know, Amy."

"It's simple. Cinderella is supposed to be beautiful and glamorous," Lila explained. "And long hair is more beautiful." She flipped her long, light-brown hair over her shoulder.

4

"That's right," Jessica agreed, playing with her own long hair.

Mrs. Otis shook her head. "I'm surprised at you, girls. Who says you have to have long hair to be beautiful?"

"Because all the princesses in fairy tales have long hair," Ellen said confidently.

"Well, then, you can't be Cinderella either. Your hair is only down to your chin, Ellen," Elizabeth said. "But you're wrong, Lila. Princesses can too have short hair. Besides, this is just pretend."

Amy nodded. "I could be a great Cinderella," she said stubbornly. "It doesn't matter how you look, it matters who you are."

Lila laughed. "No. You've got it wrong. If you're beautiful and glamorous, people will like you better."

6

Their teacher looked startled. "That's very interesting, Lila. As Amy said, I always thought it was the beauty inside that counts."

Jessica began to get an uncomfortable, itchy feeling. She knew Mrs. Otis wanted to teach them a lesson. She knew she should say that she agreed with Mrs. Otis, even though she didn't. "I believe that, too," she fibbed.

"Do you, Lila?" Mrs. Otis asked.

Lila glanced at Jessica and then shrugged. Jessica could tell Lila didn't believe it either. "Well . . . I guess so," Lila said, crossing her fingers behind her back.

Mrs. Otis smiled. "That's good to hear. I'm glad we had this little talk," she said as she walked over to the seesaws.

"See?" Amy said. "Now I can be Cinderella."

"No, you can't," Lila replied.

"But Mrs. Otis said—" Elizabeth began.

"I don't care what Mrs. Otis said," Lila insisted. "Cinderella has to have beautiful hair. And right now I have more beautiful hair than Amy. So I'll be Cinderella."

Amy looked furious. "Then I hope you turn into a pumpkin!" she shouted, before running away.

CHAPTER 2

Party!

Elizabeth began to follow Amy to the jungle gym, but Jessica stopped her.

"Don't go, Liz," Jessica said. "Stay and play with us."

"I don't want to if Lila is going to be so mean," Elizabeth said.

"Please?" Jessica begged. "It'll be fun."

Elizabeth hesitated. She and Jessica almost always played together during recess. "Oh, all right," she agreed, looking one last time toward Amy.

"Good," Jessica replied happily. They walked back to Lila and Ellen. "Let's pretend it's the prince's ball, and Cinderella is going to go."

"What kind of gown are you going to wear?" Ellen asked Elizabeth.

"A blue one," Elizabeth answered. "And it has to have pockets."

Lila giggled. "My ball gown is made all of silver."

Jessica did a perfect curtsy, the way she had learned in dance class. "I wish we really had a fancy party to go to. Nobody in our class has had a birthday party or anything in the longest time."

Lila spun around. "Oh, did I forget to say that *I'm* having a fancy party?" she announced unexpectedly. "On Saturday."

Everyone stopped and stared at her. "This Saturday?" Elizabeth asked.

"Yes," Lila said, twirling her hair around one finger. "It's going to be really fantastic, with clowns and pony rides. I'm inviting the whole class."

"Why didn't you tell us before now?" Jessica asked.

Lila shrugged. "I didn't want to, that's why."

"What's the party for?" Ellen asked eagerly.

"It's not your birthday," Elizabeth reminded Lila.

"Saturday is April first. The party is for April Fools' Day," Lila told them. She looked around the playground and smiled a satisfied smile. "It'll be the best party anybody around here ever saw."

Elizabeth wanted to tell Lila to quit boasting so much, but she didn't want to be rude. "That's nice," was all she said.

"Can we go swimming in your

swimming pool?" Ellen asked.

"Oh, sure," Lila said airily. "There's even going to be one of those blow-up castles to jump around in."

"Wow." Ellen looked at Lila with admiration. "That sounds so cool. Can I tell everyone?"

"Sure. Tell them they'll miss the best time ever if they don't come," Lila said as the bell ending recess rang.

They all headed inside the school building. "Lila sure is a show-off," Elizabeth whispered to Jessica.

"I know, but so what?" Jessica whispered back. "It sounds like a super party. Now we have a reason to get all dressed up."

Elizabeth rolled her eyes. She didn't like wearing fancy clothes much. "I'm going to spend most of the party in the pool," she said.

As they filed into the classroom, Mrs. Otis waved the girls over to her desk.

"I'd like to ask your opinion," their teacher began. "Especially Lila's and Jessica's and Ellen's."

Jessica raised her chin proudly. "Sure, Mrs. Otis. What is it?"

Their teacher smiled and tapped her chin with one finger in a thoughtful way. "I was thinking about what you girls said at recess," she explained.

"About Cinderella?" Elizabeth asked.

"That's right," Mrs. Otis said. She took a small mirror out of her desk drawer and fluffed her dark hair as she looked at her reflection. "I'm thinking about dyeing my hair red, like Caroline's."

Elizabeth's mouth dropped open in shock. She glanced over at Caroline Pearce, whose hair was bright red. "Why?"

"I think it would make me look more glamorous," Mrs. Otis said. She looked at Lila and Jessica. "I think you might be right, after all."

"Really?" Lila asked uncertainly.

"Sure. I don't want to grow my hair long, but I can make it a more exciting color," Mrs. Otis said.

The girls were all silent. Elizabeth couldn't believe what she was hearing. She noticed that Amy looked surprised, too.

"But you're perfect the way you are," Elizabeth said.

Mrs. Otis chuckled. "That's sweet of you, Elizabeth, but after all, looking attractive is important. You girls said so yourselves. I think I'll do it."

CHAPTER 3

Something's Wrong

Jessica jumped off the last step of the school bus behind Lila. Elizabeth followed more slowly, and all three began to walk up the long gravel driveway to the Fowler mansion. Jessica often played at Lila's house after school, and today, Elizabeth had to also. Their mother was taking their older brother, Steven, on a clothes-shopping trip. Steven had said, "I don't want any baby sisters tagging along."

"What should we do first, Lila?" Jessica asked as they stepped through the front door into a marble hallway. Lila's house was the fanciest one Jessica had ever been in.

Lila dropped her book bag on the floor. "How about a snack?"

"Yes, please," Elizabeth said. "I'm really hungry."

With a majestic wave of her hand, Lila led the way to the kitchen. Jessica followed close behind. She loved visiting at Lila's house, and playing with all of Lila's expensive toys.

"Well, hello, girls," said Nica, the Fowlers' cook. "You look like you could use some nourishment." She held up a large platter of cookies. "Fresh-baked peanut-butter-and-chocolate-chip cookies just for you."

"Mmmm!" Jessica said, grabbing a handful.

"Thank you," Elizabeth said as she

16

munched. "They're delicious."

Nica poured out three glasses of milk. "I always like to see you twins, you're such nice girls," she said with a friendly smile.

"Then it's lucky for you that you get to see us again on Saturday," Jessica giggled.

"What do—" Nica started to say.

"These are good cookies, Nica," Lila interrupted. Her face was starting to turn red. "I wish you'd bake them more often."

"Why, thank you, Lila," Nica replied.

Jessica frowned into her glass of milk. Was it her imagination, or had Nica seemed puzzled when Jessica mentioned Saturday?

"Come on," Lila said, pushing back her chair. "Let's go up to my room."

Jessica and Elizabeth followed behind Lila as she led them up the wide staircase. "Nica will be making all kinds of cakes and cookies for Saturday," Lila said over her shoulder. "There's going to be a cook-out and even a cotton-candy machine."

"Oh, I love cotton candy," Jessica said. "I'll get a pink one."

Elizabeth smiled. "Remember, Mom usually makes us share one," she reminded her sister. "She says it's too much sugar for one person."

Lila opened the door of her bedroom. "I always get my own. My parents let me do whatever I want," she boasted. "Whatever I ask for, they get it for me. That's why I'm having this party. Do you like my new dollhouse?"

Jessica felt a pang of jealousy as she examined Lila's dollhouse. She and Elizabeth had one at home. Jessica loved to play with it, but Lila's was much fancier. It was three stories high, and already filled with furniture.

"Do the lights work?" Elizabeth asked, kneeling down and touching a tiny lamp.

"Of course," Lila said. "My father wanted the best kind of dollhouse for me. He bought it on one of his business trips to England. You know, he's going to have a playhouse built next to the swimming pool, just for me."

Elizabeth smiled mischievously. "Maybe it will be a gingerbread house, like Hansel and Gretel's!"

"If that's what I wanted, he'd get one," Lila said, laughing.

Jessica picked up a miniature Oriental rug and stroked the velvety pattern. She was getting tired of hearing about how Lila could do or have whatever she asked for.

"I'm going to get some more cookies," she said, getting up suddenly and going to the door.

She glanced back once. Elizabeth was listening with a polite but bored expression as Lila named all her dolls. Jessica slipped out of the room and ran down the stairs.

"Nica?" she called out, walking back into the large, modern kitchen.

"Hi," Nica answered, coming out of the walk-in pantry.

"I came for more cookies," Jessica explained as she helped herself. "They're really good."

"Thank you," the cook said. She wiped her hands on her apron and poured another glass of milk for Jessica, then picked up a cookie to eat herself.

Jessica munched in silence for a moment. She had a sneaking suspicion

21

that something wasn't quite right.

"Are you going to make more of these cookies for the party?" Jessica asked finally.

Nica swallowed her bite of cookie. "What party?"

"On Saturday," Jessica said slowly, beginning to frown. She took a sip of milk. "You know, Lila's April Fools' Day party with the clowns and the pony and everything."

"I haven't heard anything about a party," Nica replied. "Mrs. Fowler is away for the month, and Mr. Fowler hasn't said a word to me. Maybe Lila meant someone else is having a party."

"I don't think so," Jessica said, setting her glass of milk down with a thump. "But I'm going to find out."

CHAPTER 4

The Truth

Elizabeth stole a look out the window as Lila picked up another expensive doll. The sun was shining on Lila's swing set, and Elizabeth wished she could go outside to play instead of listening to Lila brag.

"This doll was made in France," Lila said. "It's very delicate. So I can't let you hold it."

"That's OK," Elizabeth said truthfully. "I don't mind."

Just then the door burst open. Jessica stood in the doorway with her hands on her hips.

"You're not having any party on Saturday!" she said, staring straight at Lila.

Elizabeth gasped in surprise and looked at Lila. Lila's face was slowly turning red for the second time that afternoon.

"I am so having a party," Lila said.

"Then how come Nica doesn't know anything about it?" Jessica demanded.

"Because . . ." Lila looked down and fidgeted with her French doll. "Because I haven't . . ." Her voice trailed off in a mumble.

"You haven't what?" Elizabeth asked.

Lila defiantly stuck her chin in the air. "I haven't exactly asked my father yet," she admitted. "But since he always says yes, I know I can have the party."

24

"Oh, brother." Jessica shook her head. "I knew I shouldn't have believed you. You were making all that stuff up."

"I was not," Lila said. "Don't worry. There's going to be a party. And it's going to be great."

After dinner back home, Elizabeth and Jessica sat in the kitchen to do some finger painting. Mrs. Wakefield was working on a design for her interior-decorating class.

"Lila is just a big faker," Jessica grumbled as she smeared a red streak across her paper.

"She's such a show-off," Elizabeth said. "She made up the party just so she would be the center of attention."

"Made up what party?" Mrs. Wakefield asked.

Elizabeth explained what had happened on the playground and then again at Lila's house. "Now we don't know if there really is going to be a party or not," she concluded. She added more yellow to her painting.

Their mother set down her pencil and ruler. "There's only one way to find out," she said, reaching for the phone. Elizabeth and Jessica watched in silence as Mrs. Wakefield opened their phone book and punched in a number. "Hello, may I speak to Mr. Fowler, please?" Mrs. Wakefield asked.

"She's calling Lila's father!" Jessica whispered to Elizabeth.

As Mrs. Wakefield talked to Mr. Fowler, the twins listened to every word. Elizabeth was sitting on the edge of her chair.

"So you haven't heard anything about it?" Mrs. Wakefield said. "I see.

Yes." Their mother listened to Mr. Fowler for a moment. Then a smile spread across her face. "Yes, I see. Well, that should certainly do the trick," she said.

Jessica almost fell off her chair. "What is it?" she burst out.

Elizabeth brought one gooey, paint-covered finger to her lips. She tried to lean close to her mother to hear, but Mrs. Wakefield shook her head.

"That's fine, Mr. Fowler," Mrs. Wakefield said, still smiling. "Thank you for clearing this whole thing up. Good-bye."

With a chuckle, she hung up the phone.

CHAPTER 5

Mr. Fowler's Plan

Jessica jumped out of her chair. "What is it?" she begged. "Please tell us!"

Part of her hoped that Mr. Fowler had canceled the party. That would teach Lila not to brag about how spoiled she was. But Jessica also wanted a fancy, exciting party to go to. She held her breath, waiting for Mrs. Wakefield to explain the intriguing phone call.

"Is Lila having a party?" Elizabeth asked.

Mrs. Wakefield gave them a mysterious smile. "The answer is . . . yes and no."

"What does that mean?" Jessica demanded impatiently.

"Well," their mother said, sitting back down at the table. "Mr. Fowler has a plan."

"What kind of a plan, Mom?" Elizabeth leaned across the table on her elbows, just as full of curiosity as Jessica.

"Lila's father is very upset that she would tell everyone about a party without asking his permission first," Mrs. Wakefield told them. "So he wants to teach her a lesson."

Jessica's eyes sparkled as she slipped back into her chair and traced her fingers lightly on her paper. "What's he going to do?"

"He's going to tell her that she can't

31

have the party," Mrs. Wakefield said.

"You're kidding!" Jessica almost clapped both hands over her mouth, but remembered the paint just in time. She wasn't sure if she was happy or disappointed. "It serves Lila right for being such a show-off," she said.

"Boy, is she going to be embarrassed when she has to tell everyone there's not going to be any party," Elizabeth added.

Mrs. Wakefield held up one hand. "But wait—there is a party."

"Huh?" Jessica blinked in confusion. "I don't get it."

"Mr. Fowler wants to teach Lila a lesson, but he doesn't want her to be completely miserable. So he's going to give a party for the whole class on Saturday," their mother said. "But it will be at the beach. And it will be a surprise for Lila. It's his April Fools' joke."

Elizabeth's eyes widened. "Wow. That's a little bit mean, but nice at the same time. It's a good April Fools' joke."

"Mr. Fowler said for you to let everyone in class know what's really happening, but not until Friday," Mrs. Wakefield said. "He doesn't want you telling people before then in case someone spills the secret to Lila."

"We won't," Jessica and Elizabeth said at the same time.

"I can't wait until tomorrow," Jessica added. "I wonder what excuse Lila will give for not having the party."

CHAPTER 6

Lila's Circus

At recess the next day, many of the kids gathered around the swings to ask Lila about her party. Elizabeth sat on an empty swing and pumped back and forth slowly, wondering what Lila would say.

"Somebody told me there are going to be pony rides," Julie Porter said excitedly. "Are you really having ponies, Lila?"

"Oh, yes," Lila replied.

"I heard there was going to be a lion tamer," Eva Simpson said.

"And a trapeze artist too," Todd Wilkins added.

Elizabeth looked at Lila. She was surprised that Lila hadn't told their classmates that her father hadn't even said she could have the party. But maybe Lila was just trying to get up the courage to do it. Elizabeth knew it would be hard for Lila to admit she couldn't *always* do *exactly* what she wanted.

"Yes, we're also having a carousel," Lila went on as more kids in their class gathered around. "And there'll be a donkey."

"A donkey! Hey, listen to me!" Winston Egbert, the class clown, said. "Hee-haw, hee-haw!"

Ken Matthews laughed. "With your big ears, you even look like a donkey," he said.

36

"That's not all," Lila said, raising her voice for attention. "There's going to be a magician!" she said loudly.

"A magician! Cool!" Ricky Capaldo said. "Maybe he can make someone disappear."

"If I say so, he will," Lila said with more and more certainty. "And there will be prizes for the winners of the games, and four kinds of fancy cakes. And ice-cream sundaes too."

Elizabeth couldn't believe her ears. She watched and listened as Lila gave more and more details for a party that wasn't going to happen. She couldn't understand it. Last night, it had seemed very clear that Mr. Fowler was going to teach Lila a lesson. Elizabeth doubted that he would have changed his mind. At last, when Lila came to sit on a swing, and the other kids left to

play kickball, Elizabeth decided to find out the truth.

"Did you talk to your father?" Elizabeth asked Lila in a puzzled voice. "Did he say you can have the party?"

"Oh—well—you know," Lila stalled, pumping her legs hard. She swung past Elizabeth, back and forth. "He'll say yes," she said at last.

Lila's voice was as loud and bossy as ever, but Elizabeth could see a worried frown on Lila's face. She was sure Mr. Fowler had told Lila no. But obviously Lila wasn't going to tell anyone she couldn't have her own way!

"Maybe you should tell people it's not a hundred percent definite," Elizabeth suggested, pumping her own legs hard as she tried to keep up with Lila.

"It is definite," Lila said. "It's totally definite."

Elizabeth just shook her head.

When recess ended and everyone walked back into the classroom, Mrs. Otis waved Elizabeth, Jessica, Ellen, and Lila over to her desk. "I just wanted you to know I went ahead and made an appointment," their teacher told them.

"An appointment for what?" Ellen asked as Amy joined the group.

"An appointment at the hair-dresser's," Mrs. Otis said with a smile.

Elizabeth gulped hard. "Are you really going to dye your hair red?" she asked in a horrified voice.

"Oh, I think I could use a whole new look," Mrs. Otis said. "Amy has a whole new look, and I'd like one, too."

Jessica looked very doubtful. "Why?"

"You said it was how you felt on the inside that counts," Amy said.

"That's what I used to think," Mrs.

Otis said with a laugh. "Now I'm not so sure. What do you think, Lila?"

Lila didn't answer. Elizabeth could see that Lila was thinking—and worrying—about other things. Elizabeth thought she could guess precisely what those other things were.

Jessica nudged Lila with one elbow. "What do you think?"

"Oh, definitely," Lila said.

Mrs. Otis smiled. "I'm glad you agree."

Lila suddenly seemed to realize what she had said. "Uh, maybe—maybe you should think about it some more?" she stammered.

"No. I'm having my hair dyed on Thursday after school," Mrs. Otis said. "On Friday you'll see a whole new me."

Lila turned away. "I wish I could be a whole new me on Friday, too," Elizabeth heard Lila mutter under her breath.

CHAPTER 7

A Shared Secret

For the next two days, Lila continued to talk about her party. Jessica knew her friend was lying. Every time she asked Lila if Mr. Fowler had given his permission yet, Lila insisted that he would say yes.

"He just has to say yes," Lila muttered as they stood in the milk line at lunch. "What will I do if he doesn't?"

Jessica looked at some dishes of green Jell-O with green grapes that were on the cafeteria counter. "Look at that," she said with a giggle. "It looks like eyeballs in there. Isn't that icky? It practically makes me feel sick."

Lila suddenly froze in place. She looked at Jessica with relief in her eyes. "That's it," she said, beginning to smile.

"What's it?" Jessica asked. "Jell-O eyeballs?"

Lila smiled mysteriously. Then she raised her voice so some of their friends on line could hear her speak. "I'm not feeling very well. My head hurts, and I think I'm getting a fever. I hope I'm not sick on Saturday."

"Oh, no! Will you have to cancel your party?" Lois Waller asked Lila anxiously.

Lila shrugged her shoulders. "I don't know . . ."

"I'm sure you'll be fine," Jessica told Lila with a wide grin. She continued to smile as Lila paid for her milk and hurried away.

"Why are you smiling?" Ellen asked Jessica. "Lila just said her party might be canceled."

Jessica held back a giggle. "I have a secret. I was supposed to tell everyone tomorrow, but I can't keep it in anymore." She leaned close to whisper in Ellen's ear. "Lila's father told her she can't have the party. Lila just doesn't want to admit it. But Mr. Fowler told my mom that he's going to give Lila a surprise party at the beach. Everyone's supposed to meet there at noon on Saturday."

Ellen looked confused. "So Lila thinks she's not having a party, even though she keeps talking about it?" she asked.

"Right," Jessica said. "She doesn't

want to admit she can't always get her own way."

Ellen began to smile. Then she laughed. "Wait until the others hear this."

One by one, each person in Mrs. Otis's class was let in on the secret. By the end of lunch, everyone knew that Lila's fancy party was off, but that there was going to be a beach party instead. Amy looked over at Lila at their lunch table and let out a giggle.

"What's so funny?" Lila asked suspiciously. She put her empty milk container back on her tray.

"I'm just so excited about Saturday," Amy answered, giggling again. "I've never ridden an elephant before."

Lila bit her lip. "I might have to cancel the party. I'm feeling sick, you know."

"You don't look sick to me," Eva told

her. "You ate every bite of your lunch. Sick people don't have appetites."

"I bet your party is going to be awesome," Todd added. "I can't wait to see the lady on the flying trapeze."

Lila stood up and beckoned to Jessica. "I have to talk to you," she whispered, taking Jessica over to one side of the lunchroom. "What am I going to do?"

"What do you mean?" Jessica asked in her most innocent voice.

"What if my father never says yes? It's already Thursday." Lila gulped, and looked over her shoulder at their classmates. "How can I get out of it?"

"He'll say yes," Jessica said confidently. "He always says yes, right?"

Lila looked as though she wanted to vanish into thin air. "Maybe this time he won't," she mumbled.

"Don't worry," Jessica said even

more confidently. "I bet your party is going to be a lot of fun."

Jessica smiled again and walked back to the lunch table. She knew what she had said was perfectly true. Lila really was going to have a fun party on Saturday—but she was the only one who didn't know it!

CHAPTER 8

Mrs. Otis's Joke

Elizabeth, Jessica, and everyone else in class sat at their desks on Friday morning. The bell for the start of class had rung several minutes ago.

"I wonder where Mrs. Otis is," Jessica said, looking at the teacher's empty chair. Suddenly she slapped one hand to her forehead. "Oh no!" Her eyes were wide as she looked at Elizabeth. "She was going to—"

Just then Mrs. Otis walked into the room. At least, Elizabeth *thought* it was Mrs. Otis. A stunned silence fell over the class.

Mrs. Otis went to her desk and sat down. "Good morning," she said cheerfully.

Everyone stared at her in amazement. Nobody seemed to know what to say.

Her hair was bright red.

Smiling, Mrs. Otis patted her new hairstyle. "I think it makes me look younger, don't you agree? More glamorous too. Kind of like a princess."

Nobody answered. Elizabeth felt embarrassed and worried. She thought her teacher had made a terrible mistake.

"Ellen? Jessica?" Mrs. Otis asked. "You were the ones who said it was important to look attractive. You too, Lila."

"Yes, but . . ." Jessica trailed off.

"Aren't you sure anymore?" Mrs. Otis asked.

Lila fidgeted uncomfortably in her seat. "It's not how you look that's really important," she said.

"Oh?" Mrs. Otis seemed very surprised. "But when Amy wanted to play Cinderella, that's not what you said."

"I guess we made a mistake," Jessica said nervously.

"Maybe you were just teasing Amy a little bit?" Mrs. Otis suggested.

Ellen nodded quickly. "That's right. We were just teasing Amy."

Their teacher smiled. "I thought that was it. And you know what? I'm teasing you, too."

To Elizabeth's astonishment—and everyone else's—Mrs. Otis pulled her hair off her head.

"It's a wig!" Elizabeth shouted.

Mrs. Otis fluffed her own dark hair with her fingers, and dropped the bright red wig on her desk. "April fools!" she said.

At once, the entire class began to laugh. Elizabeth couldn't believe their teacher had been planning the joke since Monday.

"That was a good one," Jessica giggled.

"We're April fools," Elizabeth said.

"I'm one day early," Mrs. Otis admitted. "April Fools' Day isn't until tomorrow."

Jessica turned in her seat and looked at Lila. "That's right. And tomorrow is your April Fools' Day party, isn't it?"

All eyes turned to Lila. The class waited in mischievous anticipation. Lila opened her mouth, then closed it.

She straightened the pencils on her desk.

Then she shook her head and smiled. "Wrong!" she said.

"Your party is canceled?" Elizabeth asked doubtfully.

"No," Lila said, looking around with a triumphant, show-off gleam in her eyes. "I never was planning to have an April Fools' party. It was an April Fools' joke. Get it?" She laughed loudly.

Mrs. Otis shook her head sadly. "That wasn't a very nice joke to play on your friends, Lila. They were all looking forward to your party."

"Oh, well," Lila said. "I got the last laugh."

Nobody spoke. But Elizabeth saw that Todd, Ellen, Winston, and a whole bunch of other kids were trying not to smile. Then she caught Jessica's eye, and the two of them covered their mouths to keep from laughing.

Everyone knew the biggest joke of all was going to be on Lila.

CHAPTER 9

To the Beach

Jessica carefully poured herself a glass of orange juice and sat down at the breakfast table. "This is going to be the best April Fools' Day ever," she said.

"I felt bad for Lila yesterday when she made her announcement, but I still think she's lucky," Elizabeth said through a mouthful of cornflakes. "Her father is giving her a party even though he was angry at her."

"I wonder what she'll say when she finds out." Jessica grinned and took a sip of juice. "She's going to be so surprised!"

"What's the big surprise?" the twins' brother, Steven, asked as he walked into the kitchen.

"Simple. One, Lila said she was having a party," Jessica said, counting off on her fingers. "Two, her father said she couldn't. Three, he really *is* giving her a party. Four, she kept saying she was having a party even though she knew she wasn't. Five, she finally said it was just an April Fools' joke and she never meant to have a party at all. Six . . . six?"

"You ran out of fingers," Elizabeth said with a giggle.

Mr. Wakefield folded his newspaper and rubbed his hands together briskly. "Got your beach gear packed up?" he asked.

"Beach gear?" Steven asked. "Where

does beach gear fit in? Which finger was that?"

"Number six," Jessica said. "Mr. Fowler is throwing Lila a party at the beach today just so she won't be too disappointed he said no to her super-fancy one."

"Not bad," Steven said.

"Are you girls ready to go?" Mr. Wakefield asked again. "Your mother is staying here with Steven."

"Yup," Elizabeth said. "Packed and ready."

Jessica put her cereal bowl in the sink. "Ready!"

The twins climbed into the car with their beach towels and pails and shovels. "First stop, Lila's house," Jessica said.

Mr. Wakefield saluted. "Yes, ma'am."

All the way to the Fowlers', Jessica

wondered how much longer she could keep the secret. "I'm afraid I'll spill the beans as soon as I see Lila," she told Elizabeth.

"You won't," Elizabeth said. "Because you want to see Lila be an April fool as much as I do."

The car pulled into the long driveway and came to a stop outside Lila's front door. Jessica and Elizabeth ran up the steps and rang the doorbell. They stood waiting, grinning from ear to ear.

Nica answered the door.

"Hello, girls!" the cook said in a loud, friendly voice. Then she glanced over her shoulder and whispered, "Everything's all set! I made the cookies and salad, and Mr. Fowler has hot dogs and hamburgers ready to barbecue." Then she shouted, "Lila! The Wakefield twins are here!"

60

Jessica and Elizabeth went inside and waited at the bottom of the stairs. Jessica thought she would burst, but Elizabeth kept a straight face. Lila came down the steps one at a time.

"We're going to the beach," Elizabeth said. "Do you want to come with us?"

"I don't know," Lila grumbled.

"Why are you in a bad mood?" Jessica said. "It's such a beautiful day."

"Wouldn't you be?" Lila complained. "I don't know why my dad wouldn't let me have my party. He said he had to work today and didn't want to be bothered. He already left for his office."

"So come to the beach with us," Elizabeth said. "It'll be fun. Not like your party would have been, but better than sitting home alone."

Jessica turned away and coughed

loudly. She was trying very hard not to laugh.

Lila scuffed one foot on the tile floor. "Oh, all right," she said. "I'll go put my bathing suit on."

Jessica held her breath as Lila went back upstairs. She was afraid she would laugh and give away the surprise. But she controlled herself. When Lila came back, they all went out to the car.

"Hi, Lila," Mr. Wakefield said.

"Hi, Mr. Wakefield," Lila muttered.

When they arrived at the beach, Elizabeth hopped out of the car first. "Come on, let's go over to this section," she said, leading the way.

Hanging her head, Lila followed Elizabeth. Jessica brought up the rear. Over Lila's shoulder, she could see a whole gang of kids in bathing suits. It

was their second-grade class. Lila didn't notice them. She was too busy looking down at the sand and shuffling her feet.

Then Lila finally looked up. She halted in her tracks.

"Surprise!" yelled her friends.

CHAPTER 10

April Fool

Lila gaped at the crowd. Mr. Fowler stepped forward and gave her a hug.

"April fools, sweetheart," he said with a loving smile.

Everyone laughed except Lila. For a moment, Elizabeth was afraid that the surprise had backfired.

But then Lila smiled. "Dad, you're so sneaky! You didn't really say no to my party!"

Mr. Fowler chuckled. "I wanted you to realize that it's not how much money you spend on a party that makes it fun. The most important thing is having your friends around and making sure everyone has a good time."

"That sounds a lot like what Mrs. Otis was talking about," Elizabeth said to Jessica.

Jessica nodded. "I know. It's the inside that matters, not the outside."

"Now," said Mr. Fowler. "Who's ready for a game of freeze tag?"

"Me!" everyone shouted at once.

"And I'm 'it'!" Lila yelled.

Screaming and laughing, the kids raced around the beach. Lila chased them, giggling so hard that she fell down many times in the sand. After playing tag, everyone went into the water, and then it was time to cook the hot dogs and hamburgers. Mr. Fowler announced that they could all have dessert while they were waiting.

"We'll have an upside-down, backward barbecue," he said as he waved his spatula in the air.

"This is the best kind of party," Elizabeth said through a mouthful of cake.

"I have an idea," Lila said. "Let's make a huge sand castle."

"Cinderella's castle!" Jessica suggested excitedly.

At the same time, everyone looked from Lila to Amy and back again. Elizabeth wondered if Lila was still going to be bossy after everything that had happened this week.

"Amy can be Cinderella if she wants to," Lila said with a sheepish smile.

"I don't want to be Cinderella," Amy said. Then she grinned. "Yes, I do. April fools !"

*   *   *

At school on Monday, the kids told Mrs. Otis all about the beach party. Elizabeth showed the teacher a piece of smooth sea glass that she had found.

"The beach is so much fun to explore," Elizabeth said happily.

"I'm glad you all enjoy the beach so much," Mrs. Otis said with a smile. "Because we're going to have a field trip to the Wild Seashore Preserve."

Elizabeth jumped up and down. "Yay! When are we going?"

"Next month," Mrs. Otis said. "I'll be handing out permission slips for everyone to take home today."

"What's at the seashore preserve?" Jessica asked Mrs. Otis.

The teacher opened a big picture book called *Ocean Life*.

"We'll probably see different kinds of

fish and sea animals," Mrs. Otis said as she turned the book pages around so the class could see the colorful pictures. "And shells and starfish."

"Maybe we'll see a sea monster," Winston joked.

"Or a mermaid," Jessica said. "I can't wait."

What will Jessica see at the seashore preserve? Find out in Sweet Valley Kids #49, JESSICA'S MERMAID.

SIGN UP FOR THE SWEET VALLEY HIGH® FAN CLUB!

Hey, girls! Get all the gossip on Sweet Valley High's® most popular teenagers when you join our fantastic Fan Club! As a member, you'll get all of this really cool stuff:

- Membership Card with your own personal Fan Club ID number
- A Sweet Valley High® Secret Treasure Box
- Sweet Valley High® Stationery
- Official Fan Club Pencil (for secret note writing!)
- Three Bookmarks
- A "Members Only" Door Hanger
- Two Skeins of J. & P. Coats® Embroidery Floss with flower barrette instruction leaflet
- Two editions of *The Oracle* newsletter
- Plus exclusive Sweet Valley High® product offers, special savings, contests, and much more!

Be the first to find out what Jessica & Elizabeth Wakefield are up to by joining the Sweet Valley High® Fan Club for the one-year membership fee of only $6.25 each for U.S. residents, $8.25 for Canadian residents (U.S. currency). Includes shipping & handling.

Send a check or money order (do not send cash) made payable to "Sweet Valley High® Fan Club" along with this form to:

SWEET VALLEY HIGH® FAN CLUB, BOX 3919-B, SCHAUMBURG, IL 60168-3919

NAME_____
(Please print clearly)

ADDRESS_____

CITY_____ STATE _____ ZIP_____
(Required)

AGE_____ BIRTHDAY_____ /_____ /_____

Offer good while supplies last. Allow 6-8 weeks after check clearance for delivery. Addresses without ZIP codes cannot be honored. Offer good in USA & Canada only. Void where prohibited by law.
©1993 by Francine Pascal   LCI-1383-123